There's lots of clearing up to do, and
the school pets have gone missing.
Can you help me, please?

Coat

Glove

School bag

Just look at the cloakroom! The little bears have dropped some of their belongings on the floor. Can you point to where they belong?